בס"ד

Shloimie's Letter

🌷 🌷 🌷

by Freidele Galya
Soban Biniashvili

illustrations by
Michael Biniashvili

Hachai
PUBLISHING

Shloimie's Letter

First Edition - Nissan 5781 / March 2021

Copyright © 2021 by Hachai Publishing
ALL RIGHTS RESERVED

For our parents, who gave us a strong foundation passed on from their parents... and for our children, may they always build on it and bring continued nachas for generations to come. F.G.S.B. & M.B.

Editor: D. L. Rosenfeld
Managing Editor: Yossi Leverton
Layout: Moshe Cohen

ISBN: 978-1-945560-47-7
LCCN: 2020949044

HACHAI PUBLISHING
Brooklyn, N.Y.
Tel: 718-633-0100   Fax: 718-633-0103
www.hachai.com - info@hachai.com

Printed in China

Table of Contents

Meet the Main Characters

 **Shloimie Paporovich** A responsible ten-year-old who does well at school, Shloimie is an avid stamp collector and loves to play baseball with his friends.

 Hershel Smart and dependable, Shloimie's best friend is always ready to lend a hand.

 Gittel A bright eight-year-old, she wants to be part of everything her big brother Shloimie is doing.

 Ma Mrs. Paporovich is warm, capable, and proud of her Jewish home and family.

Bubby Tatty's mother who lives with the family, Bubby shares a room with Gittel. She loves feeding people and says Tehillim in her every spare moment.

 Tatty Mr. Paporovich works very hard as a presser in a clothing factory to provide for his family.

 Fetter Zalman Ma's brother lives nearby and works as a peddler.

 **Mr. and Mrs. Barclay**
The only couple on Shloimie's block to own a car, the Barclays have no children and keep to themselves.

Please note that Shloimie, his family and friends are made up characters. This story gives readers an idea of how people lived and the challenges they may have faced just after World War II.

Chapter One

CRASH!

"Shloi-mie! Shloi-mie!"

As his friends chanted his name, ten-year-old Shloimie Paporovich loosened up his pitching arm and stretched his short, stocky frame. With the weather unusually mild for fall in Toronto, it was a perfect afternoon for a game of baseball, and most of the boys from Shloimie's Talmud Torah class were there.

There were two kids on base in the empty lot, with Shloimie's best friend Hershel at bat. Hershel's round freckled face was tense with concentration. Shloimie took a deep breath and narrowed his eyes while considering his options. *Okay, it's time for a fast ball.*

Suddenly, Hershel lowered his bat and called a time out.

Shloimie looked puzzled. "What? Afraid of my next pitch?"

"Not a chance. But it's pretty late and we're all getting hungry."

He glanced around regretfully. "Okay, fine. Just one last pitch."

"Better make it a good one," said Hershel, grinning.

Shloimie straightened his cap and got a good grip on the ball. Then he wound up, pulled his arm back, and snapped the baseball toward home plate. The pitch went wild! The catcher flung himself sideways, mitt in the air, but missed. Hershel's mouth opened as the ball flew by like a missile and landed with a shocking CRASH!

The noisy players grew silent.

Shloimie's heart sank. A crash like that could not be good.

"Hershel," Shloimie said, covering his eyes, "please tell me I did not just break one

of the windows of Mr. Barclay's house."

Mr. Barclay and his wife had just recently moved into the neighborhood, into the red brick house next to the empty lot. Mr. Barclay was an impressive height, at least six feet tall, if not taller. The neighbors knew he had some kind of important job, and he always looked dignified. He and his wife were the first non-Jewish people to move to the block and they mostly stayed to themselves. They were also the only ones on the street to own a car, which Mr. Barclay polished every weekend. The kids could always tell that he was annoyed when they were playing outside and making noise. He never said anything directly to any of them, but he always had a very stern look on his face.

"Nope, you did not break one of the windows of Mr. Barclay's house . . ." Hershel answered.

"Oh, *Boruch Hashem.*" Shloimie let out a sigh of relief.

". . . but, you did break one of the windows of Mr. Barclay's car," Hershel concluded.

"Oh no!" Shloimie groaned. "Not Mr. Barclay's car!"

One by one, the Talmud Torah boys joined the huddle around Mr. Barclay's dark grey Chevrolet. As always, the car was sparkling clean, but – to Shloimie's horror – the side passenger window had shattered into a spider web pattern that spread all across the glass. The ball itself was nowhere to be found.

An uncomfortable silence fell over the group. As if on cue, every single boy had to hurry home at that exact moment. Nobody wanted to be around for Mr. Barclay's reaction to the damaged car.

Hershel patted Shloimie on the back. "I'd better go, too. It sure is getting late."

"You're leaving?" Shloimie squeaked. "I was going to ring my neighbor's bell and tell him what happened. But, if I don't... I mean, it's not like anyone would tell him

I was the one who threw that pitch..."

"I know you," Hershel broke in. "You'll never feel right if you don't tell him the truth. Besides, this whole street is filled with Jewish families. Imagine what he'll think about Jewish boys if you don't. Want me to come with you? You threw that pitch to me, so I guess it's partly my fault."

Shloimie shook his head. "You're a good friend, Hershel. But I'm the one who threw that ball. I'll have to pay the price. The thing is, our teacher said 'Gam zu l'tova,' that everything is for the best, remember? What could possibly be good about this?"

"I don't know," Hershel said, "but I'm still coming with you."

"You're a real pal," Shloimie said. "I'm glad I don't have to do this alone."

His chest felt stiff, as if he couldn't take a full breath. This was a disaster. All Shloimie could think was "My parents can't afford to fix this broken window!"

Back in Poland, before the Second World

War, Shloimie's father had owned a grocery store. But then the family moved to Toronto when Shloimie was just a baby. They'd spent all their money on tickets to Canada, leaving no money to start a business. They were all grateful Tatty found a job in a clothing factory.

Now he spends long days pressing suits and dresses on a steaming hot garment press. Shloimie knows his father is trying to save up to rent a store of his own, but it is taking a very long time.

Gittel, his younger sister, was born in Canada, and Bubby, his father's mother, lives with them, too. With five people to provide for, Tatty has to work very hard. They need food, coal, and other things, like new shoes for Rosh Hashanah. Ma saves every penny she can, and they never go hungry, but still, there's never extra money. Shloimie sighed. *How could there be anything good about breaking Mr. Barclay's car window?*

His gloomy thoughts were interrupted when Hershel pointed his thumb toward

Mr. Barclay's house. "Let's get this over with."

Shloimie looked around at the deserted lot, which just a few minutes before had been filled with all his friends. He sighed again. *If only I hadn't thrown that last pitch.*

With heavy steps, the two boys went up the path to the red brick house and wiped their feet on the mat. Shloimie's mouth felt dry. *Hashem, please help me find the right words!*

He rang the doorbell and stepped back, holding his mitt behind him. After what seemed like a long time, the door opened, and Shloimie found himself staring directly at Mr. Barclay's shiny black shoes. His eyes traveled upward to Mr. Barclay's fancy leather belt, his silk tie, his crisp suit jacket, his stern jaw. At that moment, Mr. Barclay seemed to grow taller, and his broad shoulders filled the entire doorway.

Looking down at the two boys he asked, "May I help you?"

Shloimie tried to sound confident and friendly, but his voice came out in a whisper.

"Hello, sir." Mr. Barclay just nodded.

"Umm, my name is Shloimie Paporovich. I live just a few houses down from you, on the first floor."

"Yes," Mr. Barclay said, nodding again.

Shloimie gulped. "Well, you see, I was playing baseball with my friends just now, and I was the pitcher. My friend here was at bat, and I guess I threw the ball a little too hard, because it went way past the spot where we were playing, and it well, it, uh . . ."

"Speak up, young man," Mr. Barclay interrupted. "I can barely hear you."

Shloimie began again, trying to keep it simple, trying to get the words out. "I was playing ball with my friends, and I accidentally broke your car window. I'm sorry, Mr. Barclay."

Shloimie held his breath. *Would his neighbor be furious? Would he start yelling?*

"You broke one of my car windows," Mr. Barclay repeated. "Let's go take a look."

Mr. Barclay took a moment to put on his hat and coat. He stepped onto the porch and motioned for Shloimie and Hershel to come with him to the curb. Walking around his car, he checked it from all angles, inspecting the smashed window.

The boys followed his every move, waiting to see what would happen.

Mr. Barclay bent down, reached under the car, and pulled out the baseball that had caused all the trouble. He straightened up and held out the ball to Shloimie.

"Young man," said Mr. Barclay, "you'll need this back if your pitching is going to improve." The boys looked at each other in shock. Mr. Barclay didn't sound as angry as they had expected. He didn't sound angry at all!

Shloimie gripped the ball and stared at his neighbor. "I... I'm so sorry. I mean, thank you."

Mr. Barclay gave a tight smile. "Believe it or not, I was quite a pitcher in my day. Next time you have a game, just ask me to move my car first."

"We will... I mean, I will," Shloimie stammered. "And I will pay for a new car window, every penny!"

For the first time, Mr. Barclay looked pleased. "Do you have a plan?"

"Well, I've been saving up to buy a stamp book for my stamp collection. I can give you that money right away."

"How much have you saved up so far?" Mr. Barclay asked.

Shloimie gulped. "The last time I counted it, twenty-eight cents."

"That's a start," said Mr. Barclay, "but not nearly enough. Replacing a car window costs over five dollars. That's a lot more than a stamp book."

Shloimie's face turned pale. Five dollars was more money than Shloimie had ever seen in his life. It was a whole day of Tatty's weekly earnings!

Hershel noticed his friend's shock, and he spoke up. "I was at bat when the accident happened, and Shloimie and I, we're best friends, so I want to help. I can give you two weeks' allowance – that's ten cents!"

Mr. Barclay's mouth twitched. "You are a good friend. But thirty-eight cents is a long way from the total."

"Well," said Shloimie, his heart pounding, "what if I work it off? I'll rake your leaves, wash your car, and when winter comes, I'll shovel your sidewalk and clear a path to your front door."

"I'll help, too," Hershel added.

Mr. Barclay thought for a moment. "It's a deal, but under one condition. You must tell your parents and get their permission."

"Oh, I will. I'll tell them. And I really am sorry," Shloimie said. He felt as if a huge weight had been lifted from his chest. *There was a way to fix this!*

As Mr. Barclay strode back toward his front door, the two boys just stood there, side by side. Hershel exhaled a huge sigh of relief. "You were so brave, Shloimie!"

"I guess so. But I still can't see how any of this is good at all... breaking a window, giving up our money, having to work just to pay him back..."

Hershel laughed. "I can think of one good thing! After facing Mr. Barclay, telling your parents should be easy!"

Chapter Two

The Strange Letter

Shloimie came in through the back door and hung up his jacket. The good smells coming from the kitchen meant that Rosh Hashanah preparations were underway. Bubby was busy rolling dough for *lokshen* and *kreplach*. She was not very tall, but somehow, everyone looked up to her. Bubby's bright blue eyes twinkled at Shloimie from behind her glasses. Her loving look made him feel relaxed and glad to be home.

Ma's usually serene face creased into a frown. "Shloimie, what took so long? I expected you a while ago. There's so much to do; Rosh Hashanah is tomorrow night!"

He took a deep breath. "Sorry, Ma. There was a little accident at our ballgame, but no one's hurt, *Boruch Hashem*."

Shloimie thought for a moment about whether he should tell her now about Mr. Barclay's car window, but he didn't want to say anything in front of Bubby or Gittel – especially not in front of Gittel. He would tell Ma later on, in a private moment. She was busy checking the pantry shelves and didn't ask what had happened. For now, Shloimie gave a sigh of relief.

Then he turned to his little sister and said, "What are you doing?"

Gittel was only eight, but eager for Shloimie to treat her as an equal. With pride, she answered, "I'm chopping up the gefilte fish for Ma."

"What? A little thing like you?" Shloimie teased. "Let me take over; I'll bet your arm's sore."

Gittel rubbed her arm and shook out her hand. "I'm fine. Besides, it's almost ready, right, Ma?" Her hazel green eyes filled with hope. She really was getting tired of chopping.

Ma looked at the pile of fish in the big wooden bowl and shook her head. "A little bit more, please. The gefilte fish holds together much better when it's finely chopped."

Gittel's brown curls danced along with the chopping motion as she continued her job.

"You wanted me for something, Ma?" Shloimie asked.

"Oh, yes, Shloimie, I need you to run over to Kensington Market."

Gittel looked up, her eyes sparkling. "Ma, may I please go with Shloimie? The fish is almost finished now."

Ma shook her head. "Not today, Gittel. I need you here at home."

Gittel went back to chopping fish, but without as much enthusiasm as before.

Ma wiped her hands on a red and white checkered dish towel and then handed Shloimie some money from her change purse. "I need some carrots and beets, and Northern Spy apples for some pies. Please try to pick the very best you can find. You can take the streetcar back."

"Sure, Ma," Shloimie said. "What about honey? Do you need me to get some?"

"No, your father picked it up on his way home from work yesterday so we could make honey cake."

"Tatty's been working late every night for weeks."

Ma nodded. "If Tatty is busy pressing garments, that's a good sign. It means now that the war is over, stores are ordering dresses and suits again. It means people are able to buy new clothing for Rosh Hashanah."

Shloimie knew Ma was putting on a brave face, especially in front of Bubby. It was hard for all of them when his father came home late, so tired, his back and arms aching. But it was especially hard for Bubby to see her son working that hard to provide for his family and for her.

Bubby cut a large slice from the honey cake that was cooling on the counter. She placed it on a small glass plate and set it on the table. "Here, *yingeleh*. Before you go, have this."

"Thanks, Bubby!" Shloimie poured himself a tall glass of milk and made a *brocha* on his snack. The sticky cake was warm and fragrant with cinnamon, a real Rosh Hashanah treat. Shloimie savored every bite and then said *Al hamichya*.

His mother smiled. "Your bubby really takes care of you. I'm sure she'd like to give you more. But it's time to go! And please, don't take too long at the market."

"Okay, Ma, I'll hurry back."

With a wave to his mother, a smile for Bubby, and a wink to Gittel, he was off.

* * *

Kensington Market was always a busy place, but before every Jewish holiday, it was especially busy. Shloimie looked up and down Spadina Avenue in both directions. The sidewalk was packed as people rushed about getting ready for the new year. Men and boys were lining up for haircuts in the barber shop. People were coming out of the clothing stores with their purchases. And, of course, many shoppers were carrying bags of groceries.

Shloimie went straight to the fruit and vegetable stand. Bushels overflowing with fresh produce lined the sidewalk. He picked out a dozen shiny apples, a few big bunches of carrots and some dark purple beets. After paying, Shloimie made his way to the nearest streetcar stop.

He loved riding the streetcar. Partly like a bus and partly like a train, it rode along on rails embedded in the road, stopping every so often to let passengers off and to pick up new ones.

All polite boys were trained to let older people sit down first, so a few stops along, Shloimie stood up to let an elderly man have his seat. The man peered at him through thick glasses, staring intently. Then, he spoke.

"*Yingeleh*, are you a Paporovich?"

Shloimie blushed. He often got that

question from older people. "Yes, I am."

The old man smiled. "I knew it! You look just like your grandfather. I knew him in Poland before the war. I was just going to bring something to your house, but now I can give it to you!"

The elderly man reached in and pulled something out of his inside coat pocket. It was a thin, white envelope.

"Please give this letter to your parents as soon as you get home. It looks like it could be important."

"Thank you, sir, I will," Shloimie said, taking the envelope from him. "Thank you very much."

As the man rushed to get off at the next stop, Shloimie glanced down at the envelope. What great stamps for his collection! They were brightly colored, with a white crown design and the word "Sverige." They certainly didn't look like the other stamps he had saved in an old tea tin.

Those came from letters Ma received

from her friend in Montreal, or the United States stamps that his father retrieved from discarded mail at work.

Shloimie studied the envelope some more. There was no return address, which was odd. Shloimie tried to make out the spiky handwriting on the front:

Mr. and Mrs. Paporovich
c/o The Synagogue
Toronto, Canada

Now Shloimie was really curious. *Why was the letter addressed in such an unusual way? Where was it from? Who had sent it?*

When the streetcar reached his stop, Shloimie put the precious letter in his jacket pocket, picked up his heavy bags, and headed home to find some answers.

Chapter Three
A New Year

Shloimie wiped his feet and went straight to the kitchen to see Bubby. She sat at the table, Tehillim in hand, murmuring the holy words. Gefilte fish was simmering on the stovetop, and a large bowl of *lokshen* was cooling on the counter.

Shloimie sat down beside his grandmother. She smiled affectionately at her grandson, continued for a few minutes more, and then closed the *sefer*. "What perfect timing, *yingeleh*. I just finished. Were you able to get everything on your mother's list?"

"Yes," Shloimie nodded, "I tried to choose the freshest." He carefully pulled the groceries out of the bags and placed the change from his pocket into a small jar next to the *pushkah*.

"Everything looks wonderful. What a good boy you are! I'm going to add these to the fish now." She stood up and pulled out one bunch of carrots. After snapping off the leaves, she started to peel a few bright orange carrots at the sink.

"Where is everybody else?" Shloimie asked.

"Gittel is busy playing with her paper dolls, Ma is downstairs, and Tatty," Bubby said, with a small sigh, glancing at the clock, "still isn't home."

"Okay," Shloimie said, clutching the letter. "I have something I need to give Ma right away."

"And now that she's alone, I can tell her about Mr. Barclay's car," Shloimie thought, heading down to the basement.

Ma was standing by the furnace, taking potatoes out from among the hot coals. She put each blackened baked potato carefully on a plate, then wrapped them up in a towel to keep warm.

Shloimie smiled. "I was hoping we were going to have baked potatoes for dinner tonight." The toasty smell made him hungry.

"Glad you're back, Shloimie. Did you give everything you bought to Bubby?"

"Yes, she's already adding carrots to the fish."

Ma took out the last potato and closed the door to the furnace. "Good. Now I'm going up to make apple pies."

Her eyes twinkled. "One won't be enough because your *Fetter* Zalman is coming for all the meals, and he really loves pie."

Shloimie laughed. His mother's younger brother really did love apple pie. He could probably finish a whole one all by himself!

"Do you want to help eat the apple peels?" Ma asked. "Or is a ten-year-old boy too old for that job?"

"I won't ever be too old for that!" He paused, running his finger along the edge of the envelope. "But... Ma, before we go upstairs, I need to tell you something."

"What is it?" Ma reached out to feel Shloimie's forehead. "What's wrong? Are you sick?"

"No, Ma. I'm fine, *Boruch Hashem.* It's about before... you know, when I was playing with Hershel and the other boys. We were playing baseball, like we always do, and..."

"Didn't you have a good time?" Ma asked.

"Well, yes, we were all having a very good time." Shloimie paused again. "But then, when I was about to throw the ball to Hershel... I mean, I was the pitcher, and I threw the ball really hard, and by accident, the ball..."

"Shloimie, where did you get that?" Ma looked sharply at the envelope Shloimie was holding in his restless hands.

"Oh, this is for you and Tatty. As I was coming home from the market, a man who knew Zaidy gave it to me. He said it seems like it could be very important," Shloimie

explained, handing the letter to Ma.

Ma passed the plate of potatoes to Shloimie so she could examine the envelope. "How unusual," she mused. "It's from someone who didn't even know our address!"

Carefully, she slit the thin envelope straight across the top. Shloimie watched her remove a thin one-page letter from the envelope. When Ma began reading, she gasped. Her forehead creased, trying to decipher the unfamiliar script. Finally she looked up, a faraway expression in her eyes and an excited smile on her lips.

"Who's it from?" Shloimie asked, unable to contain his curiosity.

Ma looked at Shloimie as if suddenly remembering that he was still standing there. Quickly, she stuffed the letter back into the envelope and put it in the pocket of her apron. "It's just a letter," she said. "Nothing for you to worry about."

Judging by the way Ma reacted, the letter did seem important. Together, they made their way up from the cellar, Ma still distracted and Shloimie, disappointed. He had so many questions, and he still hadn't told his mother what happened to Mr. Barclay's car!

"Ma, can I finish telling you about the game now?"

"You'll tell me later. We'll eat the potatoes while they're hot. Then I want to make those pies and put all the food away."

Shloimie sighed. "Okay. Do you still need someone to eat those apple peels?"

Gittel was standing at the top of the steps. "Apple peels! Can I have some?"

"Absolutely," Ma answered. "You'll eat them for dessert."

* * *

The next evening, as Bubby, Ma and Gittel lit the candles and recited the *brachos*, Shloimie felt an increased joy in the air. He watched Ma linger over the flames, eyes closed, *davening* for every member of her family. At last she opened her eyes and gave Shloimie and Gittel a hug.

"*A guht, gebentched yuhr,*" she whispered.

Gittel twirled around in her new skirt and blouse. "I can't believe it's 5707!"

Tatty smiled at Gittel's excitement. "I have a feeling this is going to be a very good year for the Paporovich family." Shloimie looked over at Tatty. Usually, his father was a man of few words, gentle and quiet. Tonight, he looked excited, standing tall in his *yom tov* clothing, his face beaming.

Everyone wished each other good *yom tov*. Then Shloimie and his father hurried down the street, met *Fetter* Zalman, and went straight to the *shul* in the Talmud Torah building. With his dark beard and broad shoulders, *Fetter* Zalman always exuded a regal presence. He never seemed like a peddler to Shloimie, but rather, like a prince.

With the next two days filled with *davening*, hearing the *shofar*, and eating delicious food, Shloimie had no time at all to think about the mysterious letter. He certainly didn't want to break the festive *yom tov* mood by mentioning Mr. Barclay's car.

Chapter Four
Where is S-v-e-r-i-g-e?

A new year always felt like a new beginning to Shloimie. After Rosh Hashanah and Yom Kippur had passed, he felt extra good inside and more cheerful about doing his chores. He shoveled coal into the bin near the furnace, ran errands for his parents, and did all of his homework.

The one thing still bothering Shloimie was that he hadn't yet told Tatty and Ma about his deal with Mr. Barclay. Somehow, he couldn't seem to find the right time. Either Gittel was right there, or his mother was too busy, or his father was working late.

Shloimie sighed. *This week, im yirtzeh Hashem. I've got to tell them this week. Or now. Maybe now would be good.*

Shloimie saw Bubby was resting in the room she shared with Gittel behind the kitchen. From the window, he spotted Gittel playing in the backyard. Quietly, he tiptoed into the kitchen where his mother was ironing his father's shirts.

"Oh, Shloimie, I'm glad you're here. I need you to run to the post office and buy an airmail envelope and some stamps."

Shloimie was about to ask why, and who Ma might be writing to in another country, but he thought he'd better not. Instead, he just said, "Okay, Ma, but before I go, can I just tell you about that baseball game?"

"What baseball game?" Ma asked, as she continued ironing.

"You know the baseball game I was playing with my friends before Rosh Hashanah? Anyway, like I was telling you that day..."

"Shloimie, would you please tell me another time? I really need items from the post office. I have to write an important letter before *yontif.*" Ma handed him some money from her apron pocket.

"Sure, Ma. I'll tell you later." Shloimie sighed and headed outside. It was one of those cold, sunny fall days, with an afternoon sky so bright and blue, it lifted his mood. He felt even better when he saw Hershel coming toward him.

"Shloimie!" Hershel called out. "Where are you going?"

"I need to get something at the post office. Why?"

"I thought maybe you were going to Mr. Barclay's house to start working for him. Did you tell your parents yet?"

Shloimie shook his head. "No, not yet. Did you?"

Hershel looked at the ground and kicked a pebble. "Me neither." He looked up at Shloimie. "When are you going to tell them?"

"This week, I hope," Shloimie said.

"I tried to tell my mother – twice – but she's really busy right now. I've got to tell her before Sukkos."

Hershel nodded. "Me, too. Say, can I tag along with you now?"

Shloimie thought for a moment. "Actually, I really wish you would. I'm kind of trying to find out something important. Maybe you can help me."

"Sure! Sounds mysterious, though."

"Not really. It all started with a letter, a letter with some really nifty stamps."

Just as he was about to explain, Shloimie heard his name being called. The boys turned around and saw Gittel galloping behind them, waving Shloimie's jacket.

"Ma said you need to take this," she gasped.

Shloimie rolled his eyes. "Okay, thanks a lot." He put on his jacket and turned back to Hershel when Gittel interrupted again.

"Shloimie, I've got news."

"What is it now?" Shloimie asked

impatiently. "I have to go."

Hershel started walking down the block, and Shloimie was anxious to leave.

"I just thought you might want to know that I heard something very interesting about Mr. Barclay's car."

Shloimie tried not to react. *What did his little sister know?*

"Like what?" Shloimie asked.

"Well," Gittel said, pleased to have her brother's attention, "it seems someone pitched a ball the wrong way, and it broke one of the windows of Mr. Barclay's car."

Shloimie didn't answer.

"It was you, Shloimie! Wasn't it? You're always the pitcher, I know it," Gittel said.

"Okay, okay. Yes, it was, but you'd better not tell Tatty or Ma, because I haven't had a chance to tell them yet."

Gittel nodded in sympathy. "Don't worry. I won't tell. But, boy! Will they be upset! How are they going to pay for something like that?"

"Hershel and I are going to work it off, doing chores for Mr. Barclay, that's how," Shloimie explained, trying to stay calm.

"Can I help too?" Gittel asked.

"We don't need any help," Shloimie said.

Gittel pursed her lips and began walking away. "Well then, I sure hope I don't slip up and mention the accident by mistake."

Shloimie panicked. "Wait, Gittel."

She stopped and turned around.

"I really could use all the help I can get. I forgot you're not little anymore."

Gittel beamed. "Thanks, Shloimie. I'll be a big help, you'll see." With that, she skipped back toward the house. Shloimie turned and ran to join Hershel, feeling his problem had gotten even more out of control.

As the boys walked along, Shloimie told his best friend all about the letter.

Hershel listened carefully. "So, the

stamps said "S-v-e-r-i-g-e?"

Shloimie nodded. Hershel thought for a minute.

"It must be the name of a place, right?" Hershel said. "So, I have an idea. We're already heading to the post office... why not ask about it there? They should know everything about stamps!"

Shloimie grinned. "Why didn't I think of that? Hershel, you're the greatest."

* * *

Shloimie opened the door to the post office, and he and Hershel took their place in line. Shloimie liked the orderliness, the quiet of the place. Everyone had something important to mail, to buy, or to take home. Yet everyone was standing politely, waiting to be served. At last it was their turn.

"What do you need, boys?" the postal worker asked.

"A thin airmail envelope and some stamps, please," Shloimie said. "And, um,

I have a question. If I've seen a stamp with the letters S-v-e-r-i-g-e on it, where is it from?"

The postal worker looked confused. "No idea. I'll ask my supervisor."

The boys waited, and waited, and waited some more. At last, the clerk reappeared.

"I'm sorry. My supervisor is on his lunch break. Why don't you come back later?"

Hershel looked surprised. Shloimie shrugged. "That's okay," he said. He paid for the items and pocketed his change. "Thanks, anyway."

"What now?" he asked his friend. Hershel paused, deep in thought. "How about our school library? Maybe someone there can give us information."

Shloimie brightened. *It was fun to be with his friend and see what they could find out. Almost like being detectives!*

"Good idea, Hershel. But school is closed until after Sukkos, and the library is locked."

Hershel sighed. "It will have to wait, I guess. In the meantime, what else can we do to earn some money... even before we start working for Mr. Barclay?"

Shloimie shook his head. "I'm all out of ideas."

"You could sell some of your stamps. I know you have doubles."

"Nah. I've only got doubles of United States stamps. They're easy to find. No one wants them."

"That's a shame," Hershel answered.

"And so is this," Shloimie said, pausing at the exit of the post office. "Look what I was saving up for... Now I'll never be able to get it."

Shloimie reached out and pulled a stamp album off the shelf. He held it in his hands for a few moments and ran his hand over the black leather cover. The word "STAMPS" was embossed in shiny gold letters across the front.

"That's a beauty," Hershel said. "Maybe someday."

Shloimie bit his lip. He looked down at the stamp book in his hands one more time before putting it back on the shelf. "There's still nothing good about any of this that I can see."

"I know what you mean," Hershel agreed. "Doesn't look good to me, either. But there must be something. We just have to find it."

"I wish I knew what it was," Shloimie sighed.

"Me, too, buddy."

As the boys left the post office, Shloimie suddenly froze in his tracks.

"What's wrong?" Hershel asked.

Shloimie gulped. "Look who's headed our way."

Before Hershel could respond, the boys found themselves face to face with Mr. Barclay.

"Hello, boys," he said.

"Hello, Mr. Barclay," they responded.

"So, I'll be seeing both of you in about a

week, after your holidays are over?"

"Yes, sir," Shloimie said.

Mr. Barclay nodded and started to make his way into the post office.

Just then, Hershel spoke up. "Uh, Mr. Barclay, would you happen to know what the word 'Sverige' means?"

Shloimie gasped and shot Hershel a look. *How could he have asked Mr. Barclay? Of all the people in the world!*

But Mr. Barclay didn't seem to mind the question.

"Sverige? That's the Swedish word for 'Sweden.' Why do you ask?"

Hershel was about to answer when he felt Shloimie step lightly on his foot. "Oh, I was just wondering, that's all. Well, thank you."

"You're welcome," Mr. Barclay said, as he entered the post office.

When Mr. Barclay was out of earshot, Shloimie hissed, "How could you have asked Mr. Barclay? What were you thinking?"

"Why not? I figured a big important guy like Mr. Barclay would know the answer – and I was right. He did know. I got us the answer, didn't I?"

Shloimie sighed. "I guess so. But for the future, let's leave Mr. Barclay out of our business, okay? That's the last thing I need – more of Mr. Barclay."

"Okay, okay," Hershel said. "But thanks to me, now we boy detectives only need to figure out one more thing…"

"What's that?" Shloimie asked.

"Who on earth would have sent a letter from Sweden to your parents?"

Shloimie shrugged. "You know, maybe this just isn't any of our business."

Hershel paused. "Really? But wouldn't it be fun to find out?"

"Maybe," Shloimie answered. "But what if it's private? I mean, maybe if I need to know, my parents will just tell me."

Hershel liked the idea of finding out a secret, but he knew Shloimie was right.

"Well, what else can we do to keep busy?"

"I don't know about you," Shloimie answered, "but I'm going to build the *shul sukkah* with my father tomorrow. And I can't wait!"

Chapter Five
Sharing Secrets

The early morning air was crisp but not too cool – perfect weather to build a *sukkah*. Shloimie lengthened his strides to keep up with his father as they walked to *shul* together. He loved spending time with Tatty, and those opportunities were few and precious. Even without talking, it was comforting just to be near his beloved father.

After *davening* was over that morning and everyone else left, they went outside and put on work gloves. Tatty's back usually hurt after a long day at work, but in the morning, after stretching and walking around, he always felt better.

Shloimie helped his father carry the heavy boards from the shed in the corner of the *shul's* property.   As Shloimie held one of the walls of the *sukkah* in place, Tatty hammered the nails to attach it to the sukkah frame. They made a good team, working contentedly side by side.

Shloimie took a deep breath. *I hate to spoil the mood, but it's now or never.*

"Tatty," Shloimie said, "do you know Mr. Barclay who lives on our block?"

His father nodded. "He and his wife live in the red brick house, right?"

"Yes.   And before Rosh Hashanah, when I was playing ball with the guys, a pitch went wild... and I accidentally... broke one of the windows of his car."

Shloimie's father looked up.   "Why didn't you tell us before?"

"I did try, but Gittel was always around, you were working late, Ma was busy..."

Shloimie's voice trailed off.   All his excuses sounded pretty weak as he said them.

Tatty didn't look angry.   He looked

worried. "How much will it cost us?"

Shloimie straightened his shoulders. "I'm taking care of it, Tatty. I'm giving Mr. Barclay all the money I've been saving up. I apologized and offered to work off my debt by doing chores for him after Sukkos. I mean, with your permission. Hershel is a

good friend, and he's going to help me."

Tatty put his hand on Shloimie's shoulder.

"*Yingeleh*, I'm sorry that the window broke, but I am pleased that you handled yourself like a *mentsch*. I will let Mr. Barclay know you have our permission to work for him, but make sure you don't neglect the chores around our house!"

"I won't, Tatty… really!"

His father looked thoughtful. "You took care of your own problem, Shloimie. You're really growing up."

Shloimie glowed. A compliment from his father was hard to earn. He picked up the next board and held it steady. He felt so light and free now that he'd been able to confide his secret.

"When will you tell Ma about this?"

"Soon, I guess, but she seems very distracted ever since she got that letter from Sweden."

Tatty lowered his hammer. "How did you know it was from Sweden?"

"I figured it out from the stamps," Shloimie answered. "They were different from any stamps I'd ever seen. I hope that was okay."

"That was fine. You really know a lot about stamps."

"I enjoy collecting all different kinds," said Shloimie. "I look at my stamps and imagine going to all those places around the world. What would it be like to go to Sweden?"

Tatty's face grew serious. "If you could travel with someone, it might be a wonderful trip. If you were there all by yourself, not so wonderful."

Shloimie thought about that. Just going to faraway places wouldn't be fun if he were all alone. He'd want to go with his family... or with Hershel.

"I guess so," he answered. "Just like building a *sukkah* wouldn't be fun by myself,

Tatty. It's only fun with you."

His father smiled and continued hammering the *sukkah* walls. The work was moving along nicely.

After a long pause, Shloimie said, "So, maybe *you'll* tell Ma about Mr. Barclay's broken window?"

Tatty looked at him. "The most important part of growing up is doing what's difficult."

Shloimie laughed. "I knew you'd say that!"

"I said it because it's true. And maybe when your mother hears how you are taking care of your own problem, she'll realize how grown up you are."

Shloimie thought about that. Maybe, when he finally told Ma what happened, she'd be so amazed at her grown up son that she would tell him about the mysterious letter. When he started remembering to be nicer to Gittel, maybe that would help, too.

With a renewed sense of purpose,

Shloimie lifted the next board. He felt strong and capable, ready for whatever lay ahead, even if it would be difficult.

* * *

Shloimie lay in his bed that night, but it seemed impossible to sleep. He'd told Ma all about the accident, and she had been more upset than Tatty. She thought there was a way to pitch baseballs more carefully. She wasn't happy that her son had waited so long before telling her what happened.

Shloimie twisted and turned, trying to get comfortable. His room had once been part of the hallway, and his father had put up a temporary wall to create some privacy. The little room was tiny and cold, but it was a place of his own. Shloimie pulled the covers up to his chin. His thoughts were going in circles.

Tomorrow, right after school, I'll be raking leaves for Mr. Barclay. Ma said there were lots of leaves in our yard, too. If I rake two yards in one afternoon, my shoulders will be sore for a week! That sure is doing what's difficult.

Voices rose and fell in the kitchen. He could hear the tea kettle whistling, and his *Fetter* Zalman's deep voice. Why would his mother's younger brother visit so late on a weeknight?

Shloimie turned toward the wall. He thought Ma would be as proud as Tatty was at the way he'd handled things. He sighed into his pillow and tried to breathe deeply. The pillow grew warm and lumpy. Shloimie sat up, punched the pillow and turned it over. It felt like he'd been lying there for hours.

Suddenly, he heard Tatty's footsteps in the hall.

"*Yingeleh*, put on your robe and come to the kitchen. Hurry."

Shloimie's stomach churned. *Am I going to be punished after all? Is Ma still upset?*

He tied his robe around the middle and slid into his bedroom slippers. All along the way, his heart was racing. A bright light shone from the kitchen, and the smell of freshly baked *rugelach* greeted him.

The adults stopped talking as soon as they saw Shloimie standing in the doorway. Ma had a brown folder with papers in front of her. Bubby was the first to speak.

"Here, Shloimie, come sit by me." Bubby had put two *rugelach* on a plate and was pouring a cup of tea for him. It didn't feel as if he were in trouble. This felt different.

Fetter Zalman smiled at him. "Shloimeleh, you're taller every time I see you!"

Shloimie blushed. Ma picked up a paper from the folder. Shloimie recognized the spiky handwriting and the thin paper. Would he find out all about this puzzling letter right here, right now?

Ma looked at him, then murmured to Tatty, "Are you sure he's not too young for all this?"

"He's growing up. He needs to know."

Shloimie didn't know what to do, so he made a *brocha* and sipped his tea. It was sweet and hot, warming him from the inside. He looked straight at Ma, and she abruptly asked him a question.

"You know I have a sister?"

Shloimie nodded. Ma had a sister he'd never met. She and her family had remained in Poland, and Ma wrote her a letter every week. Ma kept trying to convince Aunt Shaindel to come to Canada. Then, one day, the postman brought Ma's letter back. He explained that the person must have moved. She wasn't at that address anymore.

Still, for a long time, every week, Ma wrote a letter. And every time, the postman brought it back.

Gittel was too young, but Shloimie remembered Ma crying, sometimes in the middle of regular days, sometimes while washing the dishes – washing, rinsing, and crying. He could never understand why she was so sad.

At some point, he understood more. All the Polish Jews had been forced to leave their homes during the war. Even now, it was hard to know where any of those people were… or if they were okay. And from when he was small, Shloimie understood that he must never ask Ma about her family. He didn't want to make her cry.

"I know about her," he answered. "I've seen her picture."

Fetter Zalman pulled a photo out of his pocket. "Here's Shaindel with her whole family right before the war." He held it out, and Shloimie took it with trembling hands.

"That's Shaindel with her husband, your Uncle Dovid... their little baby girl, Rosa, and their older son, Leib. In this picture, he must be around twelve."

Shloimie recognized the same deep set eyes as Ma, the same determined chin. This was his cousin, before the war, before everything changed.

"Where is he now?"

Fetter Zalman pulled a checkered handkerchief out of his pocket. Shloimie couldn't believe it. His big, strong uncle was crying.

Shloimie looked at Ma. "Leib's in Sweden, isn't he? My cousin wrote that letter!"

Ma nodded. Her voice came out all soft and shaky.

"Now that the war is over, hundreds of

thousands of Jews with nowhere to go have been living in displaced persons' camps. The camps provide some food and a place to sleep. Leib lives in a DP camp in Sweden, but no one knows where the rest of our family might be. We're trying to find out, but..."

Ma didn't seem able to explain any more. She opened the folder in front of her and took out the same thin letter Shloimie had first brought home before the New Year. With a sigh, she handed it to him.

Shloimie unfolded it and read:

Dear Fetter and Mummeh,

After so long, you may be surprised to learn that boruch Hashem, I survived the war. I have delayed sending you this letter because I did not want to put any burden upon your family – but it seems that you are now the only family I have left.

I live with other Jewish men and boys in a displaced persons' camp in Sweden. None of us have anywhere else to go. It is my greatest hope that I will be able to be reunited with you and have a real home again.

If this letter reaches you, please write back when you are able. I eagerly await your letter.

Your loving nephew,
Leib

Shloimie tingled with excitement. *How neat to have an older cousin!* After the war, most of his friends didn't have any extended family at all.

Shloimie's thoughts were racing. "This is great news! I have an idea – Leib can have my bed, and I can sleep on the folding cot! How soon can he come to Canada?"

The adults were strangely quiet. Tatty cleared his throat. "Of course we want Leib to be here with us. He's family. But there's one very serious problem."

"What is it?"

"We can't seem to get anywhere with the Immigration Department," Tatty said.

"What is that, exactly?" Shloimie asked.

"The Canadian Government has a branch that has to approve the application papers of anyone from another country who wants to live or work in Canada. Leib did not get permission," Tatty explained.

"Isn't there anything we can do?" Shloimie asked.

"I don't know," Tatty said sadly. "Your mother, your uncle and I have been trying every which way to bring him here, but it's very complicated. Last week, we met with the Jewish Immigrant Aid Society to see if they could help us. There are so many rules. We're so grateful that we came to Canada years ago, before the war started."

"That's what you said today... why you said it wouldn't be fun to be all alone in a country like Sweden," Shloimie realized.

"Yes," Tatty answered. "At first your mother didn't want to tell you about a serious matter like this. But both of us agreed you are old enough to know. Please don't discuss it with Gittel. She is still too young to deal with the disappointment."

Shloimie slumped down in his seat.

He tried to look as if he could deal with disappointment, but his heart was heavy. He folded up the letter and handed it back to his mother.

"There must be something we can do. We can't give up."

Fetter Zalman wiped his eyes and put his hand on Shloimie's shoulder. "Of course we won't give up. But what you can do now is say *Tehillim* and daven that your Aunt Shaindel's boy will be with us one day."

"Now, back to bed with you," Tatty said.

Shloimie stood up and walked over to Ma. She was staring down at Leib's letter. He kissed her on the cheek and gave her a long hug. She hugged him back, her cheeks wet with tears. Then he trudged to his room, thoughts swirling around in his mind.

It is hard to grow up. It's easier not to know. But I'm glad I do. Please, Hashem, please bring my cousin Leib safely here to us!

Chapter Six
Reporting for Duty

Sukkos was over, and school had started once again. Most boys were glad to be back after *yom tov*, eager to start up their afternoon baseball games. Shloimie sighed and put his school books on the dining room table. There was a game going on right now, in front of another friend's house. He frowned. *If I miss too many games, my pitching arm will get rusty.*

Still frowning, Shloimie headed back outside. Gittel came up behind him, munching on an apple as an after-school snack.

"Where are you going?" she asked.

"Hershel and I are going over to Mr. Barclay's house to rake his leaves and clean up his yard."

"Oh, can I come?" Gittel asked. "You said I could help, remember?" Her hazel eyes looked so hopeful, so eager.

"Yes, I do remember, but raking leaves is not for you. It's hard work."

"Then what can I do?" she persisted.

Shloimie thought for a moment. "You know how it's always my job to prepare the empty milk bottles for the milkman to pick up? Well, since I'll be busy at Mr. Barclay's house, how would you like to be in charge of the milk bottles?"

Gittel's eyes lit up, her whole face beaming. "Oh, Shloimie! Really? I could definitely do that! And it would be a big help to you, right?"

"Yes, it would be a big help," Shloimie agreed. "Rinse each one in the sink and put them on the doorstep. Okay? But now, I've got to get going. I'll see you later." He dashed out the door before Gittel could change her mind.

Hershel was waiting outside for

Shloimie. "Ready?" he asked.

"Ready as I'll ever be," Shloimie said. "Thanks for helping out, instead of going to play ball with our pals."

Hurrying up the street towards the red brick house, he felt a bit uneasy. They walked up the steps to the porch. Shloimie took a deep breath and rang the bell. Within just a few moments, the door opened and the boys once again found themselves face to face with Mr. Barclay.

"Hello Mr. Barclay," Shloimie said. "We came to rake your leaves."

"Right on time! Excellent. I've left two rakes at the side of the house," Mr. Barclay said. "Let me know when you're finished, and I'll come out to see how you've done."

"Okay, we will," Shloimie said, "but before we start we wanted to give you this." Shloimie reached deep into his jacket pocket and pulled out a little bag with coins. He handed it to Mr. Barclay.

"What is this?" Mr. Barclay asked,

opening up the bag and seeing the change inside.

"It's the thirty-eight cents we had told you about before – twenty-eight from me and ten from Hershel."

"Thank you, boys." Mr. Barclay pulled a small cloth-bound notebook and a thin pencil from his shirt pocket. "I'll keep track of the money you give me and the number of hours that you work. Be sure you get all the leaves into piles – there are a lot of them, as you can see."

Shloimie and Hershel nodded and with that, Mr. Barclay closed the door.

Left alone now, the boys went around to the side of the house and picked up the rakes. Their handles were thick and made of wood, and they felt heavier than the boys expected. As they glanced around the yard, they could both see that Mr. Barclay was right; there were a lot of leaves. But Shloimie knew it would not help to *kvetch* about it. Bubby always said that when a job needs to be done, it is much better to do it with *simcha.* Shloimie pondered the task at hand and came up with an idea.

"Hey Hershel! I know what we can do! Let's pretend that we're in a contest to see who can rake the most leaves in the shortest time. Let's race!"

"It's a deal!" Hershel loved contests.

After an hour of raking the leaves into two huge piles, the boys were finally finished. "And I do believe I won," Shloimie announced, pretending to hear cheers and applause from an imaginary crowd.

"Not a chance," Hershel said. "It was a tie, fair and square, and I know how to celebrate."

He took a running leap and landed in his friend's huge pile of crunchy leaves.

Shloimie laughed, dropped his rake, and dived into Hershel's pile.

Both boys sat up, covered in leaves from head to toe.

Shloimie pulled a leaf from his cap.

"I am not doing all this work over again. Let's rake the damage and call it a day."

"Sure," Hershel agreed. Quickly, they raked the leaves that had scattered. After looking over the lawn, they were satisfied that the job was complete. They returned the rakes to their spot and rang Mr. Barclay's bell again. Mr. Barclay opened the door.

"We're finished, Mr. Barclay," Shloimie said. "Do you want to check to make sure we did a good job?"

"Yes, I do. Let's go see." Mr. Barclay went down the steps of the porch and inspected the lawn carefully.

"You boys did a very good job, I must admit," Mr. Barclay said. "I'll burn those piles before it gets dark." He took out the notebook, wrote something and said, "That's five cents for each pile of leaves. Well done."

Shloimie sighed. If not for the broken car window, he and Hershel would each have some money to take home and save. But at least they had begun paying off that broken window!

Mr. Barclay put the notebook back in his inside coat pocket.

"Boys, don't forget to come at the same time tomorrow evening. My car needs to be washed. There's a certain way I like it to be done, and I'll show you then."

Shloimie and Hershel nodded. "We'll be here, Mr. Barclay. See you."

The two of them lingered on Mr. Barclay's front walk, pleased with their work.

"It looks really neat," Hershel said, admiring the lawn.

Shloimie looked at his palms. "Next time, let's wear work gloves. I've got a blister from all that raking."

"Is that why you look sort of down all of a sudden?"

Shloimie shook his head. "I was just thinking about something else, something that's on my mind..."

"You mean, having to rake your own yard now? I'd love to help, but I have that same job waiting for me back at my house."

"It's not that," Shloimie began.

"Then what?"

Shloimie sighed. "You know that mysterious letter from Sweden?"

"Sure!"

"Well, my parents told me who sent it."

"Really? Who?" Hershel could barely contain his curiosity.

"I can tell you, but you have to keep it quiet. My sister is too young to know, and I'm not ready to share with the rest of our class."

Hershel looked serious. "I won't say a word, Shloimie, honest. Now, who sent that letter?"

Behind the boys, a window opened, but they were too engrossed in conversation to notice.

"It's from my older cousin, Leib. He survived the war, and my parents are trying to bring him here to live with us."

"That's great news, right?"

"Well, it's great that he found us,"

Shloimie said. "But he can't come into Canada unless the government okays it first. To me, it feels like the whole country doesn't want him. My parents keep trying, but they don't know what to do next."

Hershel put his arm around his friend. "I don't know what to say. I'm really sorry. It would be so nice for you to have him here... almost like having an older brother."

Shloimie blinked hard and swallowed. He couldn't believe Hershel understood so well.

"You've got to be the best friend anyone could have. See you tomorrow, *im yirtzeh Hashem*. Same time, same place!"

"Sure!" Hershel answered. "Everything is fun when you do it with a friend... even raking."

Shloimie laughed. "Even car washing!"

As Hershel waved goodbye and headed home, Shloimie caught sight of a tall figure through an open window at the red brick house. Mr. Barclay was just standing there, staring out, a thoughtful expression on his face.

Did he hear what we were saying? Shloimie shivered in the afternoon air. *Enough of this! I can't wait until I finish paying for that car window.*

* * *

Entering through the back door, Shloimie expected to see Ma in the kitchen, but Bubby was home alone with Gittel.

"Where's Ma?" Bubby was sitting in the dining room, reciting *Tehillim*.

"She had to run an errand with Tatty this afternoon. They should be home very soon," Bubby said.

"With Tatty? He took time off work?" Shloimie asked. "Tatty never misses work, even when he's not feeling well. It must have been very important."

"Yes, it was," Bubby acknowledged, without revealing anything more.

"Where did they go?"

Bubby tilted her head slightly toward the dining room table, where Gittel was working on a puzzle. "It's not for little ears to hear about."

Shloimie understood. It must be something to do with Leib. He walked over to his little sister.

"Hi, Gittel. How are those milk bottles? And how's the puzzle coming along?"

"Milk bottles are all set. The puzzle... not so great. There are a lot of flowers in this one. The colors keep mixing me up!"

Shloimie frowned and squinted down at the table. "Look! I think this piece fits in the corner."

"You're better at everything than I am," Gittel complained. "I give up."

"You can't give up, kid. Try starting with the edges first. Then fill in the rest."

"There are five hundred pieces. I'm never going to finish."

Shloimie smiled. "Why not try looking at the lid? Then you can see the whole picture to help you."

It occurred to Shloimie how much better life would be if there were a finished picture somewhere of how things would turn out. Would that picture have Leib in it, living with them, happy in his new home? Shloimie certainly hoped so. So many pieces had to fall into place for Leib to be able to join them.

Just then, the door opened, and Shloimie's parents came in.

"Well?" Bubby asked.

Tatty shook his head, but didn't say anything. Ma didn't elaborate, either. She just looked around and murmured, "I'm going to get dinner started." She went into the kitchen, and they all heard her pulling out some pots and pans.

Bubby turned back to her *Tehillim* with a sigh.

Shloimie looked over her shoulder and said some *Tehillim*, too. For now, it was the best way – the only way – he could help his cousin in a faraway land.

Chapter Seven
Snow Days

Before long, all the leaves had fallen to the ground, and the cool autumn air was replaced by the whistling winter wind and the first snowfall of the season. It was steamy and warm in the kitchen on the last morning of Chanukah. Ma was fixing oatmeal for breakfast, and Bubby was heating milk for cocoa to celebrate the first snow day of the school year.

While he waited, Shloimie counted the Chanukah *gelt* he had... ten pennies from Tatty, and five from *Fetter* Zalman. He stacked the coins on the edge of the kitchen table, just to admire them.

"That's more than you got last year," Gittel said. Still in her nightgown and bathrobe, she yawned and took out her own handful of *gelt*.

"I only have five cents left," she sighed. "I spent the rest on a new pencil case."

Shloimie sighed too. "It's not what it seems, Gittel. My money goes to Mr. Barclay, anyway."

Every time he and Hershel had raked leaves, washed the car, or scrubbed the front porch, Mr. Barclay or his wife would let the boys know how much money their work was worth. Then the couple would subtract that amount from the price of the broken car window. So far, they'd worked off almost half the money Shloimie owed.

Gittel shook her curly head. "What a shame. You could have bought some neat stuff... marbles, a set of jacks and ball... hey!"

"What?"

"I just thought of a way to do something for you, Shloimie. Here's three more cents to give to Mr. Barclay. You'll be paid up in no time!"

Shloimie smiled. *What a cute kid. It's sweet of her to plunk down some of her own Chanukah gelt, just to help me out.*

"Thanks, Gittel. That's a swell thing to do. I won't forget it."

Ma smiled at the two of them as she dished out the oatmeal and sprinkled it with cinnamon and sugar. "What are your plans for the day? There's plenty of time to clean your rooms."

"I wish I could," Shloimie answered. "Mr. Barclay is going to need me to shovel his sidewalk and the path to his front door. Then I'll need to do the same for us. I'm glad Hershel can make it today. It's too much for one person."

Ma nodded. "You certainly have your work cut out for you. Finish your oatmeal. It will give you energy."

"And drink this," Bubby added, placing steaming mugs of hot cocoa on the table.

"Thanks, Bubby." Shloimie smiled. Bubby's hot cocoa was the best!

After dressing in his warm socks, waterproof leggings, sweater, jacket, scarf, gloves, and a warm hat with earflaps, Shloimie grabbed a snow shovel and headed over to Mr. Barclay's house. The sun glinted off the frozen, snow-covered landscape, making him squint.

Hershel was waiting for him, holding his own shovel. A thick, striped scarf completely covered the entire lower part of his face. In a muffled voice, he said, "Hi, Shloimie! Which one do you want to tackle first, the sidewalk or the path to the front steps?"

"Either way, this will take us at least an hour."

Hershel nodded. "Let's start on opposite ends of the sidewalk and meet in the middle."

"Great idea!"

The two boys began scooping up heavy shovels full of snow and ice, clearing the sidewalk bit by bit. With no distractions and just the occasional sound of the wind blowing,

Shloimie's mind filled with thoughts of his cousin Leib. How was he managing during the winter in Sweden? Did *he* have boots and a warm coat?

After close to half an hour of steady work, Shloimie looked behind him. The wind had blown a thick coating of snow back onto the sidewalk. At this rate, they wouldn't even be finished in time for dinner. And how would he shovel all that snow in front of his own house after this?

All of a sudden, Shloimie felt like crying. Everything was just too much to handle: not knowing how his cousin was doing, owing Mr. Barclay all this money, keeping up with his schoolwork... But, of course, he couldn't cry in front of his best friend.

Hershel must have read his mind though. "I bet it's even colder in Sweden where your cousin is. How is he doing?"

Shloimie shrugged, not wanting to look directly at Hershel. "Honestly, my parents don't talk too much about him – at least not to me, they don't. I know they write letters sometimes, but it doesn't seem like there's been any news."

"Why don't you write to him, too?" Hershel suggested.

Shloimie stopped shoveling and looked at his best friend. "That's a great idea, if my parents would let me."

"I'm sure they will," Hershel encouraged. "I bet he'd love to hear from you."

With renewed energy, Shloimie and Hershel got back to shoveling and before too long, had finished the job. They knocked on Mr. Barclay's door to let him know, and he promptly opened it.

"We're finished Mr. Barclay," Shloimie said. His fingers were starting to feel numb with cold, and his throat was dry.

The tall man looked outside. "Well done, boys. Mrs. Barclay will be pleased to see that the path has been cleared. That's five cents for each of you. I'll record it in the book."

"And here's some holiday money I got as a gift." Shloimie couldn't help sighing as he handed over his Chanukah *gelt*. "There's fifteen cents from me and three from my kid sister."

"And a nickel from me," Hershel added, pulling off his glove and reaching into his pocket.

Mr. Barclay allowed himself a small smile. "Thank you. I'll add all that to your account."

Shloimie nodded. "My grandmother says we're supposed to get another heavy snowfall by the end of the week, so I guess we'll be back in a few days."

"Very well. If it snows, I'll expect you then." Mr. Barclay went back inside his house.

The boys headed home with their shovels, ready to tackle the snow in front of their own houses. There was more hard work to be done.

* * *

Shloimie pulled off his waterproof boots and left his scarf and gloves to dry on the radiator. His socks were soaking wet and his face felt numb.

His father was in the living room, going over some papers. Shloimie didn't want to disturb him but Tatty heard him come in. "Back from shoveling? How was it?"

Shloimie rubbed his cold hands together for warmth. "Well... good practice for doing what's difficult. It's really cold out there!"

Shloimie's father gave him a proud look and turned back to his stack of papers.

"What are you working on, Tatty?" Shloimie pointed to the folder on the table. It looked like the one full of documents about his cousin Leib.

His father winced and stood up to stretch his back. "Just . . . thinking."

"I've been thinking, too. I've been thinking about Leib."

Tatty sighed. You have a good heart, *yingeleh*. I know you worry about him."

"Do you and Ma write letters to him?"

"Every week. Your mother and I want him to know he has a loving family waiting for him. If only our government would be more open to accepting Jewish survivors... if only they would give them a chance to build a life here in Canada."

"Would it be all right if I wrote something to Leib, too?"

"Certainly. You can add a message on the bottom of our next letter." Tatty smiled at Shloimie and held out an envelope... the envelope with the very first letter from Leib. "You can even keep the stamps from Sweden. But before you do anything, change out of your wet socks. We don't need you to catch a cold now."

"Thanks, Tatty!"

Shloimie went to his room and changed into warm, dry socks and pants. He grabbed the tea tin that held his precious stamps and hurried to the kitchen. He filled the kettle and put it to boil on the stovetop.

The steam from the kettle would make the stamps easier to peel off the envelope. As he steamed and peeled, Shloimie thought about what he would write to his cousin. He couldn't think of anything. Leib was already eighteen. Maybe he wouldn't care about what his younger cousin had to say.

Shloimie carefully removed the Swedish stamps and placed them into the tea tin that held his collection. Then he went back to the dining room.

Tatty brought out an aerogramme letter that was almost full of writing. At the bottom, there was a small space left for Shloimie's message. What should he tell Leib?

Suddenly, Shloimie thought of his father's words. *We want him to know he has a loving family waiting for him.* After tapping the pen against the table a few times, Shloimie began to write.

Dear Cousin Leib,

Hi! How are you? I am 10 years old, and in grade five at my school. I have a little sister,

Gittel, who's 8. I like to collect stamps, and my father said I could keep the ones from your letters. My parents are doing everything possible to bring you over to Canada to live with us. I already have a plan to make my room into our room. I can't wait to meet you! Please write back.

Your cousin,

Shloimie

When Tatty read Shloimie's letter, he pulled his son into a warm hug. "It will give him hope to read this. You're a good boy, *yingeleh*. A good boy with a good heart."

Chapter Eight
All for Nothing?

Winter in Toronto was always cold, and the winter of 1947 was no different. The city was completely covered in a sparkling blanket of snow. Both horses and cars struggled to move along the uneven and bumpy roads, and many cars were stuck. But those were grown-up problems.

Most children loved the snow! The streets were theirs, with lots of chances to go sledding and tobogganing. Winter meant happiness to the children of the city, but not to Shloimie. Every heavy snowfall meant only one thing to him: more shoveling at Mr. Barclay's house.

Sometimes Shloimie felt as if that broken car window would never be paid up. It was the biggest nuisance, the most horrible thing Shloimie could imagine. Hershel tried to help him most days, but he couldn't come every time.

"Oh, c'mon, Shloimie," Hershel urged him one afternoon after a particularly heavy snowfall. "We're going over to Queen's Park to build snowmen and forts. It's going to be great. You can shovel the snow afterwards."

Shloimie shook his head. "I'd love to, Hershel. You know I would. But I just can't go with you. It's going to take me the rest of the day just to finish Mr. Barclay's sidewalk, and I still have to shovel at my house, too. You go ahead. It sounds like fun."

"Okay, Shloimie," Hershel said, "suit yourself. But if you change your mind, you know where to find us."

Shloimie watched Hershel run off to join the rest of the boys from the block. He felt very sorry for himself as he trudged along towards Mr. Barclay's house, his shovel over his shoulder.

I'm the only boy who can't build a fort or play with his friends. I'm the only boy in the world, all alone with this job that will never end...

Shloimie stopped his stream of sad thoughts all of a sudden. He knew someone lonelier, someone really far away: Leib. Somehow, after remembering that, he couldn't help but grow more thankful. *I have my family, a nice home, a hot dinner waiting for me... and from all this shoveling, I must have really strong muscles by now!*

He grew more cheerful, humming as he worked, moving the shovel in time to the tune. It seemed as if those grateful thoughts helped the job go faster, and before long, the sidewalk and the front path were clear.

Breathing hard in the cold air, Shloimie bounded up the front steps and rang the bell. But after a few moments, no one came to the door. That was odd. If Mr. Barclay was still at work, Mrs. Barclay would open the door and record the amount he'd earned in the little account book. Shloimie rang again. He shifted from one foot to the other, but no one seemed to be there. Finally, he headed home.

Gittel met him at the door, her eyes wide, and her curls bouncing as she talked.

"Did you hear what happened to Mr. Barclay?"

"No, what happened?" Shloimie asked.

Gittel took a deep breath before she made her important announcement. "Mr. Barclay was hit by a car when he was crossing the street. He was taken to the hospital in an ambulance! It must have been *awful*."

"How do you know? Are you sure?"

"Yes, I'm sure. *Fetter* Zalman was there when it happened, and I was there when he told Ma. He said two men carried Mr. Barclay on a stretcher and lifted him into the back of the ambulance."

"Was he very badly hurt? Which hospital did they take him to?" Shloimie asked.

"I don't know," Gittel said, frowning. "But I bet I could find out."

"That's okay," Shloimie answered.

Gittel held out a bag of marbles. "Want to play with me, Shloimie?"

Shloimie shook his head. He was a bit shocked at the news and not at all in the mood for a game of marbles. "Not now, Gittel." He brushed past her and went to look for Ma.

It was funny. Mr. Barclay certainly wasn't his friend, but over the past few months, Shloimie had spent a lot of time doing chores for him. Shloimie felt like he should do something, but he didn't know what.

Ma stood at the stove, stirring something in a big pot.

"There you are, Shloimie. I'm sure Gittel told you the news about our neighbor."

"She sure did. But she doesn't know anything useful, like which hospital he's in or how he's doing."

Ma looked serious. "I'm sure Mrs.

Barclay went straight to the hospital when she heard what happened. As soon as she comes home, we'll go over and bring some of this nice hot chicken soup. We'll find out everything then."

Shloimie felt the tightness in his chest relax. There was something he could do. But was it enough?

His thoughts were interrupted when Gittel ran into the kitchen, her eyes wide.

"I just saw Mrs. Barclay come home in a taxi."

"Thank you, Gittel," Ma said. She carefully poured some hot soup into a jar and added lots of chicken and vegetables. Then she wrapped it in a dish towel and gave it to Shloimie to carry.

Ma put on her coat and gloves to pay their neighbor a visit. She made her way down the street with Shloimie following behind her. "The front steps are free of snow, thanks to me," he thought. "I wonder if Mrs. Barclay will realize I was working here today for over an hour."

Ma rang the bell and they waited. Within just a moment, Mrs. Barclay opened the door. She looked a bit surprised to see the two of them standing there.

"Hello," she said. "Won't you come in?"

"Maybe another time," Ma answered. "We just came to tell you how sorry we were to hear about your husband's accident and to bring you some hot soup. I'm sure you have no strength to start cooking now."

"That's so considerate of you, Mrs..."

"Paporovich," Ma said. "I'm Shloimie's mother. How is your husband doing?"

Mrs. Barclay sighed deeply. "We are so grateful that it wasn't more serious. The doctors say he is going to be all right, but they want to keep him for a few days just to make sure."

"That's very good news," Ma answered.

Shloimie got up the courage to add, "And please tell Mr. Barclay I wish him a speedy recovery."

Mrs. Barclay smiled, but her eyes looked worried. "I will. I'm going back later to bring him a few things for the night. I'll be sure to tell him... and to give him some of this nourishing soup."

As she thanked them again and gently closed the door, Shloimie's worst fears were confirmed. *She didn't even notice all my work.*

As they headed home, Shloimie heard a familiar voice calling him. It was Hershel.

"Hi Shloimie, I just saw you leaving Mr. Barclay's. What took you so long?"

Shloimie sighed. "I finished a while ago, but I had to go back."

"Why? And why did your mother go with you? Are you in some kind of trouble?"

Shloimie told his friend all about the accident and how things had changed. For once, Hershel was stumped.

"So, now that Mr. Barclay is in the hospital, and Mrs. Barclay will be going to visit all the time, there's no one to keep track of our work? So much shoveling, and it's all for nothing?"

"In a way, I guess," Shloimie answered. "And it's no one's fault. Mr. Barclay has to recover, and Mrs. Barclay is too worried to remember to write it down when she gets home. I just can't ask her... not now."

"Well, maybe you can just drop it for a while. I mean, who's going to notice if you don't show up to shovel?"

Shloimie thought about that. *Maybe I could take some time off, build snow forts with my friends, and have some good snowball fights.* But deep down, Shloimie knew he could never do that. He'd be letting Mr. Barclay down. He'd be letting himself down.

"Hershel, whether it's written down or not doesn't matter. I have to keep doing the work."

"Why?" his friend asked.

"Because it's the right thing to do," Shloimie said simply.

Hershel gave a sad smile. "You'll be working for the Barclays forever, you know that? But I'll still help you when I can."

"Thanks, buddy. See you tomorrow!"

Shloimie climbed the front steps and made his way into the house. The delicious smell of chicken soup filled the hall, and he couldn't wait to taste it.

Shloimie pulled off his gloves and laid them on the radiator to dry. He left his boots at the front door and hung up his coat. As Shloimie passed the hall table, he noticed a letter with Swedish stamps, a letter from Leib! Would there be a message for him in that letter? Shloimie knew he'd have to wait for his father to come home and open it. Tatty and Ma always read those letters together and kept them in the brown folder.

When his father finally came home, Gittel was already sleeping. The rest of the family gathered at the table while Tatty took a knife and slit the envelope from side to side. He read the letter with Ma, then passed it to Shloimie.

"There's a special message for you at the bottom, *yingeleh*. Leib wrote back to you."

Excited, Shloimie took the thin sheet from Tatty's hand and began to read.

Dear Shloimie,

I was so glad to get your letter, especially the part about sharing a room. I feel so welcome already! You also wrote that you have a stamp collection. Guess what? I used to have a stamp collection, too... before the War, of course, when I was about your age. I had some great stamps from different countries. I kept them in a stamp album that my father bought me as a birthday gift. When I get to Toronto, will you show me your stamp collection? I can't wait to see it. Most of all, I am looking forward to meeting you very soon, with Hashem's help.

Love,
Leib

Chapter Nine

Catching Up

As much as everyone wanted winter to be over, winter was staying – and nobody wanted it to be over more than Shloimie. Shoveling the snow was hard enough, but shoveling without anyone even knowing was brutal. But like Mrs. Barclay had said, Mr. Barclay's accident was not too serious, and he came home just a little over a week later. Shloimie and Hershel were there the day after he came home, clearing the path after yet another heavy snowfall.

"This snow is endless," Hershel said.

Shloimie shivered in agreement. "True but why do we always complain? We know that winter means snow in Toronto. Besides, we're not the only ones in the world with snow. In Sweden, they have snow too."

Hershel rested his arms on his shovel. "How is your cousin doing? You don't talk about him too much. Is there any word on whether he can move here yet?"

Shloimie shook his head. "He's stuck there for now, and there doesn't seem to be much we can do. The government doesn't want to let in any Jews at all."

"Yeah, but my parents said it could be they'll change the rules and start to let some survivors in."

"I'll believe it when I see it," Shloimie said. His shoulders sagged, and he swallowed hard to keep his voice from breaking.

Hershel pointed to the Barclays' house. "I think I saw Mr. Barclay by the door. He might be coming out to talk to us. Let's get back to work."

Shloimie looked toward the house. Hershel was right. The door swung open to reveal Mr. Barclay, wrapped in a scarf against the cold, with a wooden cane in his hand.

"Welcome home, Mr. Barclay," Hershel said. "How are you feeling?"

"Much better, thank you. I was very fortunate. The doctor recommended a walk around the block to get the muscles moving properly again, so here I go."

Hershel began shoveling his part of the sidewalk, and Shloimie turned to begin working on his part. But Mr. Barclay wasn't finished.

"Is something troubling you, Shloimie? You don't seem in good spirits today."

Hershel and Shloimie exchanged glances.

"Uh, no, everything's fine, Mr. Barclay. We were just talking about . . ." Shloimie wasn't sure what to say.

"About snow . . . and rules," Hershel blurted out.

"Snow and rules?" Mr. Barclay asked, confused.

"Shloimie was telling me that there's also snow in Sweden."

"In Sweden," Mr. Barclay repeated. "I suppose that's true."

"Shloimie has family in Sweden," Hershel offered.

Shloimie looked at his best friend. *Why would he tell Mr. Barclay that?* "Well, not a whole family," Shloimie corrected. "Just a cousin of mine, by himself. That's all."

"I understand," Mr. Barclay said. To Shloimie, at that moment, it seemed that Mr. Barclay really did understand. "And what was this talk about rules?"

Shloimie gulped. "Uh, well, just that the government it seems has a lot of rules about who can move to Canada . . ."

Mr. Barclay looked at the boys for a moment. "There *are* a lot of rules in the government. Rules and laws are important. But sometimes, new attitudes give way to new policies, eventually."

The boys weren't sure how to respond.

Nervous with the silence that stood between them, Shloimie said, "Anyway, we better get back to work. We still have a fair bit to go as you can see."

"Yes, I suppose you do. And I need to do my required number of steps... doctor's orders." Mr. Barclay began walking down the path to head to the street but stopped in his tracks and turned around.

"I almost forgot. It meant a great deal that you kept shoveling the snow here while I was in the hospital. Mrs. Barclay said she had no problem walking down the front path every day to visit me."

Shloimie smiled sheepishly. "I didn't mind."

"That's quite commendable of you, especially since my wife was so distracted that she forgot to record any of your work in the notebook."

Shloimie shrugged his shoulders. "That's okay. It was the right thing to do."

Mr. Barclay looked at them both intently

before he spoke again.

"Well, thank you, boys. Carry on."
And with that, he was off in his usual brisk
manner.

When Mr. Barclay was out of earshot,
Shloimie glared at Hershel.

"What was that for?" Hershel asked.

"You told Mr. Barclay I have a relative in Sweden!"

"I did, but so what? What difference does it make?"

Shloimie thought for a minute. "I guess it doesn't matter. But from now on, no more talking about anything in front of Mr. Barclay when we're over here. Okay?"

"Okay," Hershel agreed. "But I'll tell you Shloimie, when winter ends in a few weeks, we're going to have to celebrate."

"Deal, but until then, back to work," Shloimie answered.

The two friends smiled at each other.

Chapter Ten
Purim

As Shloimie sat in shul with his father and *Fetter* Zalman, waiting for the reading of *Megillas Esther* to begin, he thought about that saying his rebbi had taught the class just a few weeks earlier: *"Mishenichnas Adar, Marbim b'Simcha...* When the month of Adar enters, joy is increased."

Still, it was very hard for Shloimie to feel increased joy – let alone any joy at all – knowing that Leib was no closer to coming to Canada than he had been so many months before. Shloimie looked around the shul. Gittel and most of the other children were dressed up in costumes – Queen Esthers, Mordechais, brides, and kings – but for the first time ever, Shloimie came dressed like himself. No matter how hard he tried, he just wasn't able to get into the joyous mood of Purim.

Gloomily, he thought about Leib being so far away in Sweden. *I'm sure someone will read the Megillah in the displaced persons' camp... at least I hope so.* He sighed heavily.

Shloimie felt his father shift on the bench next to him. Tatty was not able to sit comfortably anymore. From the long hours at the clothing factory, the pain in his back had grown worse. This new pain brought more worry into their lives. *How will we manage if Tatty can't do his job? How will we get Leib to come and live with us if there's no paycheck, no money...?* Shloimie's shoulders slumped.

Hershel hurried in and plopped down next to Shloimie. He was dressed in a colorful clown suit. "Hey, it's the happiest day of the year, and you look like it's *Tisha B'Av*. What's the matter?"

Shloimie mumbled, "Lots of things are the matter."

Hershel fished a cap out of his pocket and jammed it on Shloimie's head. "There. Now you have a costume. You're a baseball player."

Shloimie grinned in spite of himself. Hershel was right. It was a day of joy, not the time for worry or sadness. Hershel grinned back and pointed to the *gabbai* of the shul, who was beginning with a speech.

"I know the hour is late, and in a few moments we will begin the *Megillah* reading, but before we do, we will be passing around an envelope for *tzedakah*. I know that I don't have to tell anyone here about the importance of the mitzvah of *matanos l'evyonim,* charitable gifts to the poor.

"The money collected will go directly to the few survivors who have been able to settle here after the war… may their numbers increase! The money will be delivered to them right away, so they will have the necessary funds to make the Purim *seudah*. We need not go back thousands of years to the story of Purim to understand our fellow Jews' plight.

"Our brothers and sisters have survived the decree of Germany's own 'Haman,' may his memory be erased forever. So, please give whatever amount you can."

When the envelope came around to Shloimie's father, he immediately reached into his pocket to give whatever he had with him. Tatty handed a few coins to Shloimie to put in, as well.

As the envelope made its way through the shul, Tatty leaned over to Shloimie. "When we came over to Canada we had very little, practically nothing. But survivors of this war have even less than we do. *Boruch Hashem*, we had each other and *Fetter* Zalman, but they have to rebuild their shattered lives.

"With Hashem's help, we will get Leib here, and at least he will have us. He will have a family to live with and even a younger brother to share a room with."

"You mean me?"

Tatty put his arm around Shloimie. "Of course I mean you, Shloimie. Leib already knows you through your letters. I'm sure you two will be very close."

The envelope had now been passed around the whole shul, and it was time to read the *Megillah*. Shloimie and the rest of the people in shul stood up to hear the recitation of the *brachos*. After hearing them and responding "Amein," they sat down and listened quietly to every word of the *Megillah*. Of course, when Haman's name was recited, everyone made noise with *graggers*, banged on the table, or stomped their feet.

Shloimie and his friends were the noisiest of all. Blotting out Haman's name had definitely taken on more meaning during the years of the war, when a modern-day Haman attempted to wipe out the Jews.

After the *Megillah* reading was over, a bunch of young boys began singing *V'nahafoch Hu*, a popular Purim song. Shloimie knew the meaning of the words: Hashem can turn any trouble or evil plans upside down, just like He did in the story of Purim – just like He did when the Second World War ended in victory.

Shloimie sang along, his happiness rising. *V'nahafoch hu – Hashem can turn anything upside down: sadness to happiness, darkness to light, far away to right nearby.*

He straightened his cap and sang

louder. For the first time in a long time, Shloimie felt the joy and confidence within him soaring and expanding. *V'nahafoch hu. He will turn it upside down! With Hashem's help, everything will work out for our family.*

Chapter Eleven
Shloimie's Letter

"So, which do you think is harder, Shloimie? Shoveling snow or doing spring clean-up?" Hershel asked, as he picked up another broken tree branch from Mr. Barclay's yard. "There sure are a lot of twigs that fell off during the winter."

"That's true, but at least it's not freezing. Give me spring clean-up any day! And I didn't mind planting Mrs. Barclay's bulbs yesterday either. It was kind of fun to mix up the earth. Once those daffodils bloom, they'll look really good, and we'll have had a part in it."

"I guess so. But don't tell me you're eager about mowing Mr. Barclay's lawn the whole summer?"

Shloimie shrugged his shoulders. "No, not really. But we'll get through it."

The boys continued working in silence until every last branch and twig was picked up from the yard and bundled together with twine. "Should we go and tell Mr. Barclay we're finished for the day?" Shloimie asked.

Hershel nodded. "And we'll also find out what needs to be done tomorrow after school."

"I don't think I can do any work here tomorrow afternoon. Pesach is less than two weeks away, and I need to be helping out at home. I think we should tell Mr. Barclay that we'll have to take a break from working at his house until Pesach is over."

"Okay," Hershel agreed. "But you can be the one to tell him."

Shloimie and Hershel went up to the porch to get Mr. Barclay to inspect their work as they had been doing for so many months. The door swung open before they had the chance to even ring the bell. Mr. Barclay seemed to be expecting them, notebook in hand. Today, he wasn't using a cane for support, and he looked very pleased.

"Hello, Mr. Barclay. We were just about to let you know we finished cleaning up the yard."

"Let me see," said Mr. Barclay, as he came down the steps. Quickly, he inspected the lawn and the bundles. "Good job," he said. He opened the notebook and turned a few pages.

"Now I'm happy to report that you boys have worked off the debt. The damage to the car has been paid in full."

Shloimie and Hershel exchanged happy glances.

Mr. Barclay closed the notebook and continued. "I'm proud of you boys. You said you would work off the debt, and you did exactly that."

"Thank you, Mr. Barclay," they answered.

Mr. Barclay nodded. "Before you go, I have something to give you, Shloimie." He reached into his jacket pocket and pulled out a sealed envelope.

"Please give this to your parents. It's very important."

Shloimie took the envelope and looked at it curiously.

"Now, you'd better be getting along." Mr. Barclay's eyes twinkled. "If you ever want to earn some spending money, you boys can do some chores for me anytime."

"We might just do that," Shloimie answered.

Mr. Barclay nodded. "Don't forget to give that envelope to your parents right away!"

Once they said their goodbyes and headed outside, Shloimie and Hershel looked down at the envelope. The outside was clearly addressed in bold typeface to Mr. and Mrs. Paporovich, complete with the address.

"Why would Mr. Barclay have my

parents' mail?" Shloimie asked.

"Maybe the mailman put it in the wrong mailbox by mistake," suggested Hershel.

"This wasn't delivered by the postal service – no stamps!" Shloimie said.

"You're right! How strange. Well, there's only one way to find out. C'mon, let's get it over to your parents."

Shloimie and Hershel hurried over to Shloimie's house. Upon entering, it was obvious that Pesach preparations were underway. Ma was scrubbing the dining room chairs, while Bubby was sweeping the carpet. Gittel was polishing the candlesticks while Tatty and *Fetter* Zalman were reviewing the *Haggadah* together. Shloimie's father had to take the day off to rest his back.

"Hi, everyone," Shloimie said. "Guess what?"

"What?" Gittel asked. She loved surprises.

"We finished paying off our debt to Mr. Barclay. No more chores at his house... unless we want to earn some spending money."

"That's wonderful, boys," Ma said, standing up.

"Well done," Tatty added. "I'm sure you thought you'd never finish."

"And now you can help us get the house ready for Pesach," Bubby joined in, smiling.

"Yes, Bubby," Shloimie said.

"What's that?" Ma asked, noticing the envelope in Shloimie's hand.

"Oh, right. Mr. Barclay gave this to me. He said it's very important and to give it to my parents." As Shloimie handed it over to his mother, he couldn't help thinking of that other mysterious letter he had given to her all those months ago – the one from Leib.

Ma looked concerned. "I wonder what this is all about." She took a knife, slit the envelope, and took out a crisp white letter on heavy paper.

As she read, her face grew pale. "Oh my!" she exclaimed. "Oh my!" She sat down abruptly in the nearest chair.

Fetter Zalman rose and took the letter from her hand. As he read, his eyes widened in surprise.

"What is it?" Tatty asked.

Ma's voice shook as she answered. "It's a letter from the Immigration Office, telling us that Leib's application to enter Canada has been approved!"

Bubby hugged Ma, *Fetter* Zalman hugged Shloimie, and Tatty clutched the precious letter tightly, tears in his eyes.

Gittel kept asking what was going on and who was Leib, until Ma took her aside and explained everything.

Shloimie stood next to his father, seeking reassurance. "Is it really true, Tatty? Can Leib come and live with us now?"

"*Boruch Hashem*, it's true," Tatty answered, handing Shloimie the letter. "See for yourself."

Shloimie took the letter and read it

slowly and carefully. It was really true! Leib would be able to leave Sweden!

"I'm so happy for your family," Hershel said. "But I have a question. Why would Mr. Barclay have this letter?"

Everyone stared at Hershel. He had a good point. What did Mr. Barclay have to do with any of this?

Shloimie looked down at the paper in his hand and gasped. "You are not going to believe it. Look who signed this." He held up the letter so everyone could see it. The signature was bold and easy to read:

William O. Barclay, Immigration Officer, Ontario, Canada.

"Mr. Barclay works for the Immigration Department?" Hershel asked in disbelief. For a moment, nobody spoke; then they all erupted in conversation, laughter, and happy tears. What an amazing turn of events! Their neighbor must have taken a personal interest in reuniting their family.

Ma wiped her eyes and stood up.

"There's so much to be done! So much to arrange for Leib. But first, we are having the Barclays over for a thank you celebration."

Chapter Twelve
New Beginnings

Ma straightened the tablecloth and rearranged the flowers for the third time that morning.

"Everything looks wonderful," Bubby said, as she placed her blueberry cheesecake in the center of the table.

"Ooh, can I have a little taste?" Gittel asked.

"Not until the Barclays arrive," Ma said.

"Well, when will they be here?"

"Any minute," Shloimie assured her.

"Thanks for inviting me to come too," Hershel told Shloimie's father.

Tatty nodded. "You're practically like

family, Hershel. You've been at Shloimie's side through all of this."

Just then, the doorbell rang.

"I'll get it," Shloimie said, hurrying to open the door. "Hello, Mr. and Mrs. Barclay. Please come in." Tatty and *Fetter* Zalman extended their hand to Mr. Barclay while Ma and Bubby greeted his wife.

"We're so happy you could come. We really wanted to thank you for what you did for our nephew," Shloimie's father said.

"I'm glad I was in a position to help," Mr. Barclay answered.

"Still, not many people would extend themselves like you did for us."

That was the final mystery that Shloimie couldn't figure out. Why had Mr. Barclay gone to the trouble of researching Leib's case? Why had he given it his close, personal attention?

"There's a reason I did it," Mr. Barclay said, as they all settled around the beautifully set table. "Do you want to know why?"

Mr. Barclay looked squarely at Shloimie. "From the day your baseball broke my car window, you took responsibility for your actions. You could have simply gone home, and I would never have known who had done the damage. Instead, you told the truth.

"I saw how hard you worked to pay off the debt, keeping at it week after week, even when your work wasn't recorded in the book. Your responsible behavior earned my respect. It changed my way of thinking. I decided that if your cousin is anything like you, Shloimie, then Canada would be fortunate to have him live here and become a contributing citizen."

Ma and Bubby wiped away tears, and Tatty's face glowed with pride.

Shloimie was speechless. He never imagined that working hard and doing the right thing could have such a powerful result. At last he understood why Mr. Barclay put effort into helping his cousin get permission to come to Canada.

Shloimie finally managed to speak.

"Mr. Barclay, you have given my family the greatest gift. Thank you."

Mr. Barclay nodded his head. "Like I said, I'm glad I was able to help. And, for your part in all this, my wife and I brought a little something just for you." Smiling, Mrs. Barclay handed Shloimie a beautiful package, covered with wrapping paper and tied with ribbon.

Surprised, Shloimie could only stammer, "Thank you, thank you so much."

"What is it, Shloimie? Open it up." Gittel never could wait when there was a gift to unwrap.

Mr. Barclay laughed. "Your sister is right. Go ahead, Shloimie,"

Shloimie's hand fumbled as he untied the shiny ribbon. Then he slit the paper to reveal what lay underneath. "It's the stamp book! The one I wanted! The stamp book I'd been saving up for before I damaged your car." He looked up, eyes shining.

"I found out which one you had your

eye on," Mr. Barclay said, winking at Hershel. "Do you like it, Shloimie?"

"Do I like it? *Do I like it?* It's fantastic! Thank you! I wanted this so badly, you have no idea!"

Mr. Barclay laughed again. "I think I have some idea. I was a ten-year-old boy once too."

Shloimie felt the heavy black cover and ran his fingers over the gold lettering. He couldn't believe the stamp book was really his. "Thank you for this great gift. It means so much to me."

"You're welcome," Mr. Barclay said, "our pleasure."

"So, *now* can we have the cheesecake?" Gittel asked.

And for the third time since coming to the Paporovich home that afternoon, Mr. Barclay laughed.

As they drank tea and ate cheesecake, the discussion turned to plans for Leib.

"As a new arrival, it's important that your nephew have a job," Mr. Barclay said. "Do you have any arrangements in place?"

They all grew quiet. Shloimie hadn't thought of that. *Would Leib be able to work in the clothing factory with Tatty? What other kind of job could he do?*

Looking over at Ma, Tatty cleared his throat. "Actually, we do have a plan."

Fetter Zalman nodded encouragingly and Bubby smiled as Tatty continued.

"I was able to find a place for rent where I can open up a grocery store. With my bad back, I'll need a strong young person to do the heavy lifting. So, my nephew will have a full-time job waiting for him."

"It sounds like a solid plan," Mr. Barclay agreed.

Ma sighed happily. "It's perfect for everyone."

"*Boruch Hashem*," Tatty said turning to Shloimie and Hershel, "but there's one more thing: we will need a few responsible boys to handle deliveries after school... when they're not busy with their studies."

The boys exchanged excited glances.

Hershel spoke first. "Gosh, thanks, Mr. Paporovich! I have to ask my parents but I'm sure they will let me. That would be great!"

"I can't wait," Shloimie added. "You can count on us."

"I know I can," Tatty said, proudly.

When the celebration was over, Shloimie walked the Barclays to the door.

Mr. Barclay held out his hand and Shloimie shook it. His neighbor looked him right in the eye. "Well done, young man. I'm sure we can all expect great things from you."

Shloimie blushed and answered, "I certainly hope so."

After the Barclays left, Shloimie thought back to the day that he broke the car window. He remembered what Hershel had told him: somehow, there is good in every single thing that happens, whether we can see it at the time or not.

"Hershel, look how many things had to happen just to get this happy ending... If I hadn't broken that window, if I hadn't been willing to walk up to that door and apologize, if you hadn't offered to do Mr. Barclay's chores with me..."

"What do you mean?" Hershel asked.

"I never would have been talking to myself! Mr. Barclay must have overheard our conversations, and then you spilled the beans about my having a relative in Sweden. It's because of every little detail that he found out about Leib in the first place, looked up his case, and then..."

Hershel broke in excitedly, "After all the people your parents asked for help, the one who had the power to do something was right there all along!"

"Only Hashem could have done this! Hashem is always looking out for us. I guess I need to remember that the next time I think that something is going wrong!"

"*Gam zu l'tova*," Hershel said, smiling.

"Told you."

Shloimie grinned. "Now, are you going to help me do one more job?"

"What's that?" Hershel asked.

"Let's rearrange my room. I can't wait for Leib to arrive!"

Author's Note

Although this book is a work of historical fiction, I was inspired to write it based on events in my own family history. All of my grandparents came to Canada from Poland between the years 1921 and 1930. My parents were both born in Toronto, as was I. When my parents went on a trip in 2017 to Halifax, Nova Scotia, they visited the Canadian Museum of Immigration at Pier 21 and were actually able to obtain printouts of the official records of their parents arriving in Canada.

When I was growing up, my parents always shared stories from their childhoods about what it was like to grow up in Toronto in the 1940's. Many of these experiences made their way into this book. Riding on streetcars, baking potatoes in the furnace, and chopping fish to make gefilte fish were strong memories that they shared with me.

But in 1939, when World War II began, I can only imagine how painfully difficult it must have been for everyone in Canada being totally helpless to rescue their family members back in Poland. They'd left behind so many siblings, nephews, nieces and many others.

One of the relatives that my father's mother was constantly worried about was her cousin, a young woman who was engaged to be married. When WWII began, it was obvious that trouble lay ahead for the Jews in Poland, so her *chosson* (groom) and his parents fled to a safer location. The chosson sent word for his *kallah* (bride) to come and join them. However, she said she couldn't do so because they were not married yet. The *chosson* wasted no time, came back to Poland, and they quickly got married.

However, as the newlyweds made their way to rejoin his parents, the borders were closed and they were trapped in Poland. Eventually, they were both deported to the concentration camps. My grandmother's cousin survived, but the young *chosson* who had come back to save her life, tragically perished.

After the war was over, this young cousin was relocated to a DP camp in Sweden. She hadn't been able to communicate with her family throughout all those years of the war. Desperate to let someone know she was alive, she thought of contacting my grandmother – but it seemed impossible. She did not have my grandmother's actual street address, and she couldn't even recall where in the world my grandmother had settled: was it Toronto, Canada or London, England?

So, she wrote two identical letters. One was addressed to my grandmother, in care of The Synagogue/Toronto, Canada, and the other was addressed in care of The Synagogue/London, England.

Miraculously, when the letter arrived at the post office in Toronto – rather than throwing it away or sending it back to Sweden – the postal service delivered it to the largest synagogue in Toronto at the time. Someone at that shul located my grandmother and gave her the letter. My grandmother opened up the envelope, stunned to hear from her long-lost cousin. The entire letter contained only three words. It read: *I am alive.*

This resourceful young woman had succeeded in letting someone know of her existence. Their family connection restored, she and my grandmother renewed a correspondence and a relationship that lasted the rest of their lives.

Unlike the happy ending in this book, my grandmother's cousin never moved closer to the family. And so, in 1968, more than twenty years after the war had ended, my father went to Sweden and met her for the first time. Years later, my sister and her husband were fortunate enough to visit our elderly cousin in Sweden as well.

Over the years, she travelled to Toronto for many family celebrations, including the weddings of my parents, my cousin, and my sister. When I was younger, I would write to this cousin regularly. She became my pen-pal, responding with letters written on beautiful cards and often containing Swedish coins for my coin collection. Just like the protagonist in this book, I enjoyed seeing the different Swedish stamps on the envelopes. Although many years have passed, I still keep and treasure all the letters she sent to me.

By the time I got married, her health was frail, and she was not able to make the long trip to Toronto again. Despite her health problems, our dear cousin had a fighting spirit well into old age. She passed away in Adar 5779 (2019), just before her 101st birthday, while this book was being edited for publication.

I am very grateful to her for telling me about the letter she sent to my grandmother so many years before. That incident always stayed with me, and I knew that one day, I wanted to write a book including a small part of her story. May her memory be for a blessing.

Historical Note

This story takes place in Toronto, Canada after the end of World War II.

When the war was over, survivors who tried to go back to their family homes or communities across Europe found they were not welcome – or that their houses and apartment buildings had been destroyed in the fighting.   Sometimes, non-Jewish neighbors had moved in and taken possession of the property and personal belongings Jewish families had to leave behind.

Survivors had no possessions, no money, no jobs, no food, and nowhere to live. They were called "displaced persons," and the facilities set up for them were called Displaced Persons' Camps or DP camps for short.

Unlike summer camps or overnight camps that are fun places to go, DP camps were grim. The authorities had to house over 11 million people, using whatever shelter was available. Cots and bunkbeds were set up in former military barracks, airports, hospitals, or even partially destroyed buildings.

It was a huge effort to feed, clothe, educate, and give medical attention to so many people in need. There were shortages of food, material for clothing, leather for shoes, and fuel for heat. Illness spread rapidly with so many people living close together. No wonder Shloimie's family was willing to do anything to bring Leib to live with them in Canada!

Survivors in DP camps had the difficult task of trying to locate family members in other countries, hoping to reunite with them. Family members in other countries, hoping to find any surviving relatives in Europe, were frustrated as well. Today, we are used to getting instant answers through computers, websites, and texts. But for survivors and their families, finding each other could take years.

The only way to research and discover information was by writing letters. Shloimie's family wrote letters to government officials, to Jewish organizations, to volunteer services, to anyone willing to help. Each letter had to be opened and read, sorted and filed, then answered by a person writing by hand or typing on a typewriter. Weeks and months could go by without a response.

Even if they found each other, some countries would not allow these families to bring in their relatives. During the Great Depression of the 1930's, fears about not having enough jobs for everyone had led to the strictest immigration laws in Canadian history. Not until May of 1947 did the government change its policies, enabling Jewish families to bring over more of their relatives who had survived the Holocaust. In the eight years that followed, the Canadian Jewish community welcomed around 35,000 survivors and their families.

After losing their homes and many loved ones, after spending time in DP camps and searching for a new place to live, survivors had to build their lives all over again. It took great strength to overcome all those traumatic experiences, but they did. They married and raised children.

They learned the language of their new country, found jobs, started businesses, and bought homes. They built shuls and strong communities. They worked hard and taught their sons and daughters to be proud Jews who would do good in the world. The strength and hope they displayed can inspire all of us to be strong and hopeful in our own lives.

Glossary

A guht, gebentched yuhr .... Yiddish for "A good, blessed year"

Al hamichya .... Prayer after eating certain foods

Amein .... Amen

Boruch Hashem .... Thank G-d

Brocha/Brachos .... Blessing/Blessings

Bubby .... Grandmother

Chanukah .... Festival of Lights

Davening .... Praying

Fetter .... Yiddish for "Uncle"

Gabbai .... Caretaker

Gam zu l'tova .... This, too, is for the good

Gefilte fish .... Chopped fish, cooked in broth

Gelt .... Money

Graggers .... Noisemakers

Haggadah .... text recited at the Seder meal on Passover

Hashem .... G-d

Im Yirtzeh Hashem .... G-d willing

Kreplach .... Dumplings

Kvetching .... Complaining

Lokshen .... Noodles

Megillas Esther (Megillah) .... Scroll containing
the Purim story

Mentsch .... Yiddish for "fine human being"

Mitzvah .... Commandment; good deed

Mummeh .... Yiddish for "Aunt"

Pesach .... Passover; Festival of Freedom

Purim .... Holiday celebrating the Jewish victory over Haman

Pushkah .... Charity box

Rosh Hashanah .... Jewish New Year

Rugelach .... Rolled pastry

Sefer .... Holy book

Seudah .... Festive meal

Shofar .... Ram's horn

Shul .... Synagogue

Simcha .... Joy

Sukkah .... Temporary dwelling in which all meals are eaten on Sukkos

Sukkos .... Festival of Booths

Talmud Torah .... Jewish Day School

Tatty .... Yiddish for "Daddy"

Tehillim .... Psalms

Tisha B'Av .... Ninth day of the Hebrew month of Av; Jewish day of mourning

Tzedakah .... Charity

V'nahafoch Hu .... "He (G-d) will turn it upside down"

Yingeleh .... Yiddish for "Little boy," a term of endearment

Yom Kippur .... Day of Atonement

Yom Tov .... Jewish holiday

Yontif .... Yiddish pronunciation for "Yom tov"

Zaidy .... Yiddish for Grandfather

In keeping with the setting and time period of the story, spelling of Jewish words and phrases is consistent with Eastern European speech, heavily influenced by Yiddish.